SMITTY

MW01178622

MOOSE

Episode Two

THE CHICKS

PETEY

AND

ME

This book is published by Lifevest Publishing Inc., Centennial, Colorado. No portion of this book may be reproduced without the expressed written consent of Lifevest Publishing or Paulette Plourde.

The Chicks is written by Paulette Plourde
illustrated by Jessica Golen
Copyright 2006, Paulette Plourde

Published and Printed by:
  Lifevest Publishing
  4901 E. Dry Creek Road, #170
  Centennial, CO 80122
  www.lifevestpublishing.com

Printed in the United States of America

I.S.B.N. 1-59879-150-8

Dedication

To my brothers -
Larry, Marc and Paul,
with whom I shared so many
wonderful adventures.

Easter Sunday was almost here
And we couldn't wait to see
What we'd find in the Easter baskets
For Smitty, Moose, Petey and me

Last year we all got a slingshot
And lots of Easter candy
We also got a new toothbrush
It sure did come in handy

Easter Sunday was finally here
So I jumped right out of bed
Tripping over my new sneakers
I fell down and hit my head

It didn't even hurt a bit
Well, maybe just a little
And there I saw beneath my rug
The knife I used to whittle

I quickly changed into my clothes
And kicked off both my slippers
I was in such a big hurry
I tripped over my flippers

I picked myself up one more time
And flew down the stairs to find
Something in my Easter basket
That just really blew my mind

It was yellow, soft and fuzzy
And I held it in my hand
I couldn't wait to tell my friends
And tripped as I tried to stand

I couldn't wait to call them up
But they beat me to the punch
They were ringing my front doorbell
Suddenly I had a hunch

They all reached into their pockets
Imagine my amazement
When each one held a yellow chick
We took them to my basement

We put them down onto the floor
And watched them chase each other
We just couldn't help but wonder
Did our chicks miss their mother

Moose came up with a great idea
And looked right over at me
He said, "Let's keep them together"
But at whose house would it be

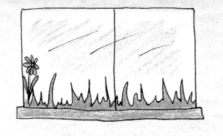

We played paper, rock and scissors
To decide whose house we'd choose
And I was the lucky winner
I was sure that I would lose

We got some hay from the pet store
And made our chicks a nice pen
One was smaller than the others
We had three roosters and a hen

The next thing that we had to do
Was give our new chicks a name
The ones that we came up with were
Rocky, Duke, Harry and Dame

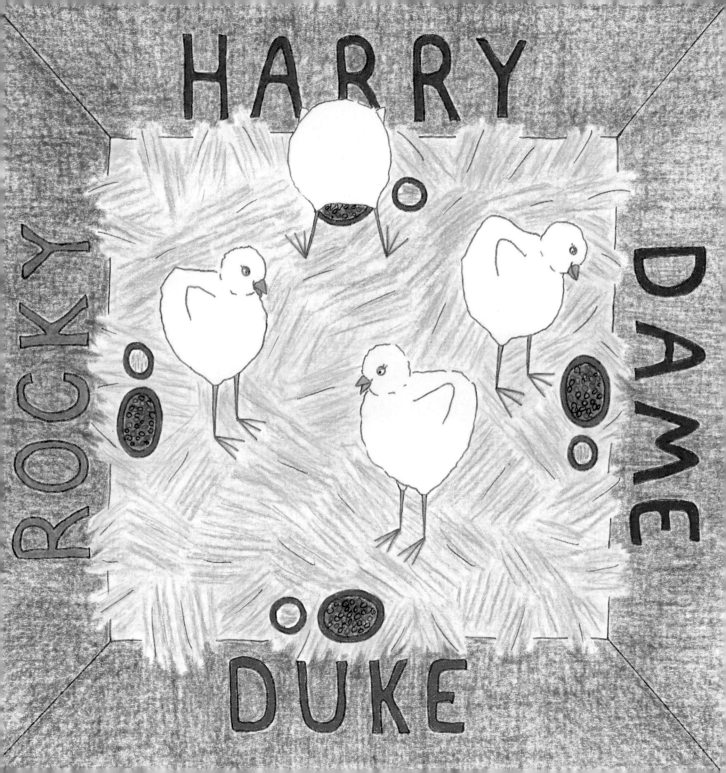

We gave them food from the pet store
Also cleaned their pen each day
We laughed as they chased each other
And loved seeing them at play

Soon their pen couldn't keep them in
As they grew by leaps and bounds
They just kept pooping everywhere
There must have been fifty pounds

My basement was getting smelly
And our chicks were now full grown
We had to make a decision
We couldn't raise them on our own

So we put our heads together
And we thought up a new plan
We'd take them to Farmer Brown's farm
For he is such a nice man

Off we all went in my Mom's car
To show Farmer Brown our chicks
He said that he'd gladly take them
And gave us licorice sticks

Farmer Brown said we could visit
We all broke out in a smile
Our houses weren't too far away
It was just about a mile

We hugged our chicks and put them down
Among the roosters and hens
And they all seemed to get along
Our chicks had found some new friends

At first we saw them once a week
And the days went flying by
We were seeing them less and less
I just couldn't tell you why

I guess we were getting older
And had other things to do
Yet every time that we drove by
We waved and I think they knew

About the Author

Paulette Plourde finds herself truly blessed with a wonderful family and friends.

Her hobbies are composing songs on the piano or guitar, gardening, writing poetry and children's stories.

Look for Episode I, *THE WITCH*

Future Episodes to Come

The Bike
The Contest
The Diamond
The Challenge
The Jail
The Raid
The Net
The Trapdoor

To Order Copies of

SMITTY, MOOSE, PETEY AND ME
EPISODE TWO:

THE CHICKS

by **Paulette Plourde**

I.S.B.N. 1-59879-150-8

Order Online at:
www.authorstobelievein.com

By Phone Toll Free at:
1-877-843-1007